Contents

Star for a Day

Jean Ure

With illustrations by
Charlie Alder

Barrington Stoke

First published in 2014 in Great Britain by
Barrington Stoke Ltd
18 Walker Street, Edinburgh, EH3 7LP

www.barringtonstoke.co.uk

Text © 2014 Jean Ure
Illustrations © 2014 Charlie Alder

A CIP catalogue record for this book is available
from the British Library upon request

ISBN: 978-1-78112-358-4

Printed in China by Leo

Chapter 1
The Curtain Rises

"Please, Mum," Lola cried. "*Please!*" She stamped her foot. "It's so not fair!"

Lola was in one of her sulks. She always sulks if she can't get her own way. She is my sister. My *little* sister. She is very spoilt.

I am Lucy, and I am not spoilt at all. I'm two years older than Lola, and nowhere near as pretty. Lola's hair is blonde and bubbly, mine is straight and the colour of mud. Lola has eyes of the brightest blue, mine are just ordinary brown. Lola is Mum's favourite. Mum calls her "my little princess". She calls me "Loopy Loo", or sometimes just Loopy.

I suppose I don't mind that much. I've got used to it. But Loopy Loo is a really stupid name for anyone over the age of five. Grandad calls me "Luce", and I like that much better. Grandad lives with us. It's just him and Mum, and me and Lola. I get on really well with Grandad.

But back to Lola and her sulks. She was bright red by now, like a tomato. Her lips were quivering, her eyes filling with tears. She is very good at crying.

"Mum?" she whispered, all pathetic.

I could see that Mum was starting to give in.

Me and Lola had been invited to a birthday party by this girl called Holly that lived up the road. She was going to be 13, the same age as me. The party was on Saturday and Lola was desperate for Mum to take her into town, like STRAIGHT AWAY, to buy her something new to wear.

"I need something, Mum! It's a *party*," she wailed.

"Well ... I don't know," Mum said. "I suppose, maybe ..."

Lola pounced. She can always tell when she is about to get her own way.

"Holly will be all dressed up," she said. "She always is!"

"It's her party," Grandad said. "When it's your party, you can be the one to dress up."

Sometimes Grandad gets a bit sharp with Lola. Mum says he doesn't understand her. Most of the time, Lola takes no notice of him. After all, what does Grandad know?

"If I can't have a new outfit," she said, "then I won't go!"

Grandad tutted.

"I mean it!" Lola screamed. "I won't go! She can, if she likes." *She* meant me. "I'll just stay home!"

Lola is always very dramatic, but it's important to her to look good. Some people like to be clever and pass exams. Some people like to be good at sport. My sister Lola likes to look pretty. It's not surprising. All her life people have told her how pretty she is. Once, when we were little and out shopping with Mum, an old lady looked at Lola and went, "Oh, how adorable!" Mum beamed and said, "She's my little princess."

Mum is so proud of her. She agrees with Lola that it's important to always look your best. And Lola knows just how to get round her.

"*Please*, Mum!" The tears were starting to trickle over and roll down her cheeks. She clasped her hands together. "Pretty please!"

Mum can never resist Lola's tears for very long. "Oh, all right," she said. "Let's go shopping!"

Chapter 2
Take Your Partner

"Hang about!" Grandad said. "What about Lucy? What's she going to wear to this party?"

Mum and Lola were already half way out of the door. They stopped. Mum looked at Grandad with a frown.

"Lucy?" she said. Like, *why should Lucy need anything?*

"She already had a new skirt," Lola cried. "Just last week!"

"That was for school," I said. School clothes don't count.

"Lucy needs something for the party too," said Grandad.

Lola pouted. "Why?"

She is the one that has to look pretty! Not me.

Grandad gave her one of his looks. He would never say so, but I think he agrees with me ... Lola is spoilt rotten.

"The trouble is," Mum said, "I can't afford to buy new clothes for both of them. Money doesn't grow on trees."

"No, and I got in first," said Lola. She looked at me in triumph.

Grandad shook his head. He beckoned to me. "Luce! Come here."

I went over to him.

"Here," said Grandad. He slipped something into my hand. A £20 note! "Take this," he said. "It should be enough to buy something nice. See what you can find."

"Lucy, what do you say?" Mum said.

"Thank you!" I threw my arms round Grandad's neck and kissed him. Grandad winked at me. We were partners.

"Can we go now?" Lola demanded. She was jigging up and down, desperate to be off. She just loves shopping for clothes.

"Lucy, I'm not taking you into town in those tatty jeans," Mum said. She gave me a little push. "Go and find something a bit more respectable."

I scampered off to my bedroom. Five seconds later, I heard Mum calling up the stairs.

"Come on, Loopy. Get a move on!"

Honestly, Mum was as bad as Lola.

I was so grateful to Grandad for giving me that money. I found a really cute top, which even Lola agreed was quite cool. Not *totally* cool. She was the only one that was *totally* cool. But cool enough to make me feel good about myself, which I don't always do and never if I have to go anywhere with Lola. Parties are the worst. Lola really sparkles at parties. She squeals a lot, and giggles a lot, and does all these little showing-off twirls, like, "Look at me, look at me!" And everybody does. She can be a bit of a pain, but people always look at her.

So there we were at Holly's place, me in my new cool top and Lola doing her thing. I was standing in a corner, watching her squeal and twirl, when this boy came up to me.

"Hi! I'm Tyler," he said. "Holly's cousin."

I felt myself blushing. Blushing is *so* embarrassing! I seem to do it for no reason at all. Why blush just because a boy starts talking to you?

"Hi," I said. I was holding a glass of orange juice. I put it up to my face and mumbled round the side of it. "I'm Lucy ... Lola's sister."

"Oh!" Tyler sounded surprised. I saw his eyes flicker across to Lola. "That's your sister?" I guessed he couldn't believe it. How could a girl that had to hide her blushes with a glass of orange juice have a sister as pretty and popular as Lola?

We stood there in silence and watched as Lola twirled. Tyler couldn't take his eyes off her. We heard the happy sound of her giggles, followed by little shrieks.

Tyler turned, at last, to look at me. "How do you –" he began, and then broke off.

"How do I what?" I said.

"Well …" He seemed a bit uncomfortable. "I don't mean to be rude. I was just going to say, how do you – I mean –" He waved a hand. "It can't be easy, having a sister like that."

I knew what he meant. It isn't always easy, having a sister who is so pretty and popular. I don't always like it very much. But before I could say anything, Lola came skipping over.

"Hey, Tyler!" she cried. She grabbed him by the hand. "Come and dance!"

She dragged him off across the room. I was left on my own, with my glass of orange juice.

At least I had my nice new top. That was something.

Chapter 3
Star Quality

"I *know* money doesn't grow on trees," Lola said. "But, Mum, I *have* to have new shoes."

Grandad rolled his eyes. "Here we go again," he said.

"No, she's right," Mum said. "She can't go for an audition with tatty old shoes that are just about falling to pieces."

Lola beamed. She had got her own way. As usual. And her old shoes *weren't* falling to pieces. They were just a bit scuffed from all the dancing she does. Ballet, for the most part. She also does a bit of jazz and tap, but it's ballet she likes best. She is really good at ballet.

"What's this audition for, anyway?" Grandad asked.

"It's for *Spotlight on Kids*," Mum said. "The talent show – on television."

She said it like Grandad should have known, but why should he? What did Grandad know about talent shows? Mum gets a bit impatient with Grandad, sometimes. He came to live with us a few months ago, after Gran had died. He'd been so lonely. I didn't mind one bit when I had to move in with Lola and let him have my bedroom. Lola grumbled, but I was just glad that Grandad wasn't on his own any more.

"Last year," Mum said, "we got through to the second round. We were Highly

Commended. Weren't we?" She beamed a proud smile at Lola.

"This year," said Lola, "I'm going to get to the finals. *If* I have some new shoes!"

"Oh, we'll get them for you," said Mum. "Don't worry. Let's see how much there is in the savings pot."

The savings pot is an old cracked vase where Mum puts her spare change. She and Lola rushed off to the kitchen to count what was in there.

"I can't help wondering," Grandad said, "just why these new shoes are so important?"

I told him how dance means everything to Lola. She's been going to dance classes since she was three years old.

"Oh, I know that," Grandad said. "But when your mum is so broke ... does Lola *really* have to have new shoes?"

"It's just for the audition," I said. "She does so want to get to the finals and be on television."

All Grandad said was, "Hm."

"She was really upset last year," I said, "when she only got Highly Commended."

I don't know why I always stick up for Lola. Perhaps some of it is just habit. But she does work hard. *Really* hard. She is very serious about her dancing. I admire her for that. Even though she is a total pain.

"How about you?" Grandad said. "Why aren't you going in for it?"

"Me?" I said. "I can't dance!"

"Who says you can't?" said Grandad.

"Lola," I said. She says I'm like a stick insect. Mum says I'm like a match stick. It's true, I'm a bit on the skinny side. Mum and Lola think it's very funny when I try to dance.

"Old Loopy's all arms and legs," Mum says.

Grandad was frowning. "I know everyone thinks your sister is talented," he said.

"She is!" I told Grandad. "Miss Andrews thinks Lola is one of the most promising pupils she's ever had." Miss Andrews is Lola's dance teacher. She once told Mum that Lola has "star quality".

"That may well be so," Grandad said. "But does it never occur to you that you might have some talent of your own?"

"Me?" I said.

It's true I do a lot better at school than Lola, but that doesn't mean I am *talented*. Just better at lessons.

"Do you remember," said Grandad, "that dance your gran taught you? The one you used to do for us when you were little?"

"Oh," I said. "The clog dance!"

Gran had been a champion clog dancer in her day. She had won medals. She'd tried to teach Lola, but Lola had never been interested. She said clog dancing wasn't *real* dancing. Not like ballet.

"You took to it like a duck to water," Grandad said. "Your gran always said that if she could have trained you up, you could have followed in her footsteps."

Gran had said that? About *me*?

"I'll tell you what," said Grandad. "I've still got your gran's old dancing shoes upstairs. Suppose I go and dig them out, and we'll see how much you remember?"

19

Chapter 4
Let the Dance Begin

Lots of people think that you wear clogs to do clog dancing. Big, clumpy, wooden clogs. But you don't. You wear shoes. Just ordinary shoes with metal bits on the bottom to make a good sound.

Gran's clog-dancing shoes were red lace-ups. They looked almost brand new. Grandad said in a sad voice that Gran hadn't worn them very often.

"She wanted me to keep them for you ... just in case you might want them," he said. "Try them on and see if they fit."

I didn't hold out much hope that adult shoes would fit me – but, oh, they were perfect!

"I thought they'd be all right," Grandad said. "Your gran was like a little sparrow."

As soon as I'd got those red shoes on I wanted to start dancing. But where could I do it?

Not indoors – my bedroom had carpet and you can't clog dance very well on carpet. There was a hard floor downstairs, but then Mum and Lola would come running to see what all the noise was about.

Grandad agreed with me. "We don't want your mum and sister finding out," he said. "This is something we'll keep to ourselves, eh? Just you and me."

I nodded. The last thing I wanted was Lola jeering at me. *Oh, look, the stick insect is dancing!*

"I know where we'll go," Grandad said. "Follow me."

I crept back down the hall after him, holding Gran's shoes in one hand. Mum and Lola were in the sitting room. They didn't hear us go past. Grandad led the way out to the garden. He pointed.

"Garage!" he said.

We shot in there like two naughty five-year-olds. Grandad switched on the light. "Perfect," he said.

Once upon a time the garage had had a car in it, but we didn't have a car any more. Mum said we couldn't afford to run it – not with all the money she had to spend on Lola's ballet classes. Not to mention all the tights and shoes and other kit she had to buy. So now the garage was just an empty space. It was perfect.

"Right," said Grandad. He moved a couple of boxes out of the way. "Let's see how much you remember."

My head didn't remember anything at all. But my feet did! They seemed to have a life of their own. As soon as they started moving, it all came flooding back to me.

As I danced, Grandad called out to me, just like Gran used to. "Step, step ... *down*. Watch that leg! Don't swing it back ... That's it, that's it, now you've got it!"

Gran had taught me several different dances. My feet were tingling with eagerness to go through them all. Grandad said we'd have to choose which one I was going to do.

"*Do?*" I said.

"For the talent show," Grandad said. "You are going to enter, aren't you?"

I stared at him.

"Come on," said Grandad. "You're a great little dancer."

But I was a stick insect! And Mum and Lola always laughed.

"If your gran were here," said Grandad, "she wouldn't take no for an answer."

But Gran wasn't here. And how could I go in for a talent show and do clog dancing? *Clogging*, as Gran used to call it. Clogging wasn't proper dancing. Lola said it wasn't. And she was the expert.

"Trust me," Grandad said. "I didn't live with your gran all those years without learning a thing or two. You've got what it takes, girl! Be brave. Let's give it a go."

I'm not really a very brave sort of person, but I'd loved Gran, and I loved Grandad. I bit my lip. I guess Grandad could see that all I needed was a little push.

"Know what?" he said. "Your gran would be so proud of you. She always said you had the gift."

"Gran said that?"

Grandad nodded. "One of the best little clog dancers around."

I felt myself grow pink.

"So how about it?" said Grandad. "How do we apply for an audition?"

I took a deep breath. "Lola did it online," I said.

"Right," said Grandad. "Let's do it!"

We had to wait till Mum and Lola went into town. They were going shopping again. This time to buy Lola a pink top to wear for her audition. As soon as they left the house, Grandad and I sat down at the computer.

"All right," said Grandad. "What do we do?"

I knew, because I had watched Mum and Lola. I typed in "Spotlight on Kids" and clicked on "Registration". A form came up and me and Grandad filled it in.

"Now what?" said Grandad.

"Look!" I pointed at the screen.

"Thank you," it read, "for registering with Spotlight on Kids. You will receive a letter in a day or two with details of where and when your audition will take place."

"What happens after that?" said Grandad. "You do the audition, and then what?"

I told him that if you got through the first round you went on to the second. And the winner of the second round went through to the finals – on television!

"So how long have we got to prepare?" Grandad asked.

The auditions were to be held at the start of July. That gave us four whole weeks. If, of course, they gave me an audition. They might just write and say they were sorry, but clog dancing didn't count. After all, it wasn't proper dancing, was it?

"Well?" said Grandad. "How long?"

"Um … four weeks?" I said.

"Plenty of time," said Grandad. "Don't look so worried … we'll get you there!"

Chapter 5
Break a Leg

My letter arrived two days later. It came flying through the door just as I was about to leave for school. I saw that it was addressed to "Miss L. French", so I pounced on it before Mum and Lola could appear. They were still in the kitchen, packing Lola's bag with her ballet things for her after-school class. Just as well! Nothing ever comes for me in the post apart from Christmas and birthday cards. Mum would have wanted to know who was writing to me.

Lola came into the hall in time to see me stuff the letter into my bag. She has very sharp eyes. They miss nothing.

"What was that?" she demanded, as we walked up to the bus stop together.

"What was what?" I said.

"You put something in your bag!" Lola narrowed her eyes. "Was it a letter?"

"Who'd be writing me letters?" I said.

"Dunno," said Lola. "But that's what it looked like."

"Apples look like peaches," I said. "It doesn't mean they *are* peaches."

I thought that was quite smart. At any rate, it made Lola think. It was several seconds before she said, "That's stupid! Apples don't look a bit like peaches."

"They do so," I said.

We argued about it all the way to the bus stop. At least it made her forget about the letter.

One of Lola's friends was on the bus. "Hattie!" Lola squealed, and she rushed off to sit with her.

I moved as far away as possible so that I could open my envelope and have a sneaky peek inside. I didn't want Lola peering over my shoulder. They might just be writing to say sorry. With a hand that was a bit trembly, I unfolded the letter.

Dear Lucy

<u>Spotlight on Kids</u>
We are pleased to inform you that your audition will be held at 3 p.m. on Saturday 6th July at the Cornflower Studios in Flower Street, Covent Garden. It should last no longer than five minutes. We look forward to seeing you.

Yours sincerely

Donna White
Spotlight on Kids

P.S. Please make sure to arrive on time.

My heart started to thump as I read it. What was I letting myself in for?

"When is your audition?" I asked Lola, as we got off the bus.

"The 6th of July," she said. "Why?"

"In the morning," I said, "or the afternoon?"

"Morning," she said. "*Why?*"

"Just wondered," I said.

At least we weren't both going to turn up at the same time. That was a relief.

Hattie linked her arm through Lola's. "What are you going to do?" she asked. "Are you going to do some ballet?"

"Yes." Lola gave a little skip and a hop. "Mum's making me a special outfit. I'm going to have a pink tutu and pink tights to go with my new pink shoes. And I've got a sparkly pink top, as well."

"All pink," Hattie gushed.

"Yes," said Lola, "cos I'm the Sugar Plum Fairy!"

When I got home that afternoon, I showed Grandad my letter.

"Good," said Grandad. "Now we're really on our way."

He said that now we had a date we must be sure to have regular rehearsals. It wasn't going to be easy cos we couldn't keep sneaking out to the garage. Even Mum would notice sooner or later. At the moment she was kept busy making Lola's costume, and Lola was kept busy with her Sugar Plum dance. She practised every day in the sitting room, with the furniture pushed back, while Mum sat in the corner and did her sewing. So long as they were busy in there, me and Grandad were able to creep off to the garage. No problem!

But I was still worried about what I was going to wear. Lola paraded in front of us in her new outfit, all pink and sparkly with her feet in their new satin slippers.

"Real pointe shoes!" said Mum. "Doesn't she look just like a proper ballerina?"

Grandad and I agreed that she did. I wasn't jealous – I really wasn't. But I couldn't help wishing that I looked like a ballerina, too.

"What am I going to wear?" I wailed at Grandad later.

"Don't panic," said Grandad. "One of the good things about clogging is that you don't have to get dressed up for it."

But I wanted to get dressed up.

"Let's see what your gran used to wear," said Grandad. He fetched down one of his photo albums and we looked at it together. "Anything take your fancy?" he asked.

"That's a nice one," I said. I pointed at a photo of Gran, which I remembered from when I was little.

"Ah, yes," said Grandad. "That was at a festival. Your gran got properly dressed up for that one."

But she wasn't dressed up like a ballerina. She just had a swirly skirt and a sparkly top. I had a skirt a bit like that – and a sparkly top. I had the one I'd bought for Holly's party.

Next day, when Lola was out at her ballet class, I stood in front of the mirror in our bedroom and tried out my skirt and top with Gran's clogging shoes. While I was studying myself, Mum came in to put some clothes away.

"Oh!" she said. "That's a pretty top. Is that the one Grandad bought you?"

Mum had seen it before, when I'd worn it for the party. But sometimes she doesn't notice what I look like.

"It suits you," she said. "Blue's a good colour for you. You should wear it more often."

I glowed. If Mum said blue was a good colour, then I knew it had to be. Both Mum and Lola are really into clothes.

"I love those shoes," said Mum. "I don't think I've seen them before. Did Grandad buy those for you as well?"

"They were Gran's," I said.

"Really?" said Mum. "I never knew Gran was so cool!"

On the day of the auditions, Mum and Lola left the house at ten o'clock.

"Isn't anyone going to say break a leg?" Lola said.

I know that "break a leg" means "good luck" in theatre speak, but I do think it's a bit odd. Why would anyone want to break a leg? Still, I said it for her, and so did Grandad.

Lola and Mum came home at lunchtime, very full of themselves.

"Honestly," said Mum, "some of the other acts were pathetic. One boy was playing the spoons, for goodness' sake!"

"And there was this girl," said Lola, "doing *street* dancing."

It seemed that street dancing was as bad as clogging. *Not real dance.* I began to wish I'd never listened to Grandad. Already I could feel my legs starting to go wobbly. By the time we arrived at Cornflower Studios that afternoon, they had almost turned to jelly.

"Grandad!" I clutched at his sleeve. "I want to go home!"

Grandad took my hand and squeezed it. "Don't you worry," he said. "You'll knock spots off 'em. Think of your gran – how happy she'd be. You can do it, Luce. Gran's the one you're dancing for. She'll be watching over you. You just get in there and do your stuff. All right?"

I nodded. I could be brave for Gran.

"Off you go," Grandad said. "I'll wait here for you. And, Luce ... break a leg!"

Chapter 6
Spotlight on Kids

I had to wait in a little side room until it was my turn to be called. Two other girls were in there. They were both older than me and obviously knew each other. They seemed very sure of themselves. As I came in, they stopped talking and turned to look at me. They watched while I took Gran's shoes out of my bag and put them on.

"Tap dancer, are you?" one asked.

"Clogger," I said.

"Clogger?" They both stared at me. "What's a clogger?"

"Clog dancing," I said.

"Oh," said the first one. She looked at the other and gave this smug nod. "Like tap for babies."

It so was *not*! But I wasn't going to argue. I was nervous enough before. By now I was almost frozen with terror. What was I doing here, with these two snooty girls? One of them had a guitar, so I thought she might be a singer. I couldn't imagine what the other one did. She was very tall and slim, dressed all in black. Black catsuit, jet black hair, thick white make-up and crimson lips. Someone called her name – "Miranda del Monaco!" – and she went swishing from the room.

"She's a Goth," said the girl with the guitar. "Cool, or what?"

I wanted to ask what she did, but my voice seemed to have gone. I opened my mouth and nothing came out. I so shouldn't have listened to Grandad!

When it came to my turn, I wobbled into the room on my jelly legs to find three people sitting there, waiting for me. One man and two women.

The man said, "Hello – Lucy, isn't it? Could you get up on stage for us?"

I wobbled up there.

One of the women gave me a kind smile. "Just start when you're ready," she said.

I wouldn't ever be ready! I wanted to go home. How could I dance when my legs were like jelly?

And then the strangest thing happened ...
All of a sudden, without any help from me, my
feet just took over. It was like they had a mind
of their own. Step, step – *down*. Step, step –
down. My feet knew exactly what they were
doing.

When I had finished, one of the women said,
"Thank you very much, Lucy. You'll hear from
us in a day or two."

I rushed out in a whirl to find Grandad.
I could feel myself beaming from ear to ear.

"Grandad, I did it!" I yelled.

"Of course you did," said Grandad. "I knew
you would. Was your old grandad right, or
wasn't he?"

I hugged him and told him that he was.

"Look at you – all excited! Really enjoyed
yourself, didn't you?" said Grandad.

I had enjoyed myself so much I almost began to hope that I might have got through to the next round. I knew it was silly, cos how could I compete with Sugar Plum Fairies and Goths?

All the same, when the letter arrived a few days later and it was for Lola and not for me, I felt a little bit shaky.

"Mum, Mum," screeched Lola. "I've made it! I'm in the next round!"

"How could you not be?" said Mum. "My little princess! Give her a big hand, everyone."

Me and Grandad both clapped. And then, without any warning, Lola let out a piercing scream.

"*M-U-U-U-U-M!*"

"What?" said Mum. "What's the matter?"

Lola thrust the letter at her. Mum took one look and all the colour drained from her face.

"*Dear LUCY?*" She snatched up the envelope. "Miss L. French ..." she read. "What's this?"

"They've made a mistake!" Lola screamed.

"But how did they get Lucy's name?" said Mum.

"They mean me, they mean me!" yelled Lola.

"But where did they –" Mum broke off.

Grandad had picked up the pile of post, which Lola had dumped on the table. Most of it looked like boring stuff. Bills and brown envelopes. Brown envelopes are always boring. But right at the bottom was another white one.

"Miss L. French?" said Grandad.

"Let me see that!" Mum tore it away from him. She ripped it open. "*Dear Lola* ... this is the one."

"So what's the other one?" demanded Lola. "What are they writing to her for?"

"It must be some kind of mix-up," said Mum.

"I don't think so," Grandad said. "Looks to me like you've got two daughters in the next round."

"*Her?*" said Lola.

"That's what it says," said Grandad.

"How can she be in it?" shouted Lola. "She didn't even do an audition!"

"Want to bet?" said Grandad. He gave me a wink.

"When did she do one?" Mum sounded put-out. She looked at me crossly. "How could you do an audition without me knowing?"

"And what could she do?" Lola said. "She can't dance! She can't sing!"

Grandad gave me a cheeky look. "Shall we tell them?" he asked.

Of course, we had to.

Lola said, "Clogging? That's as stupid as playing the spoons."

Not even Mum would let her get away with that. "I don't think that was a very nice thing to say, Lola," she said.

Lola went into a pout. "It's still not proper dancing!"

"It seems the judges thought it was," said Mum. "Oh, my goodness ... both of you in the

next round." She beamed. "What talented daughters I have!"

Mum was so excited she rang the local paper and that very same day they sent a reporter. On Friday there was a big photo of me and Lola with the headline –

SISTERS STAR IN TALENT SHOW!

I expect Lola would rather have had her picture in the paper all by herself, but she got to dress up as the Sugar Plum Fairy in her pink tutu and her pink tights, so that made her happy. Mum was proud as could be.

"Who would have thought it?" she kept saying. "Whoever would have thought it?"

"I would," said Grandad. "Well, I did," he said. "I did think it!"

Chapter 7
You Rock!

On my way home from school on Monday, I bumped into Tyler. I hadn't seen him since Holly's party. All at once I felt silly and shy and wanted to hide. But there wasn't anywhere to hide. Not unless I dived into someone's garden and crouched behind a hedge, and even I'm not that pathetic.

We met up just as I had reached our gate.

"Hi," Tyler said.

"Hi," I mumbled.

I was already starting to turn pink. But so was Tyler. I was so glad it wasn't just me.

"I've been to see my aunt," he said.

I didn't know what to say, so I just made a kind of "mmm" sound.

"Holly's mum," said Tyler.

I said, "Mmm."

"I live over that way." Tyler pointed. "Oak Avenue."

I couldn't say "mmm" *again*. So instead I said, "Oh." And then I said, "Ah."

I could feel that I was growing even pinker. Tyler was, too. I never realised that boys could blush.

"Saw your picture in the paper," he said. "I didn't know you could dance."

"Only clogging," I said. "My gran taught me when I was little."

"You must be very good at it."

I made an embarrassed gurgling sound.

"When's the next round?" Tyler asked.

"Next week," I said. "But I won't win."

"How do you know?" said Tyler.

"Cos Lola will," I said.

"Your sister." He turned from bright pink to bright scarlet as he said it. It probably meant he had a crush on her. Lots of boys do. And then he said, "I'm really sorry about ... you know. At the party. What I said."

It can't be easy, having a sister like that. That was what he had said.

"I didn't mean to be rude," said Tyler. "Honest. It was just ..."

Just that he fancied Lola. "That's OK," I said. It happens all the time.

"I know she's popular, but –" Tyler shifted from one foot to the other. What was he about to say? Was he going to ask me if I thought she would go out with him?

"She is a bit of a show-off," he said, "isn't she?"

Oh! Did that mean he *didn't* have a crush on her?

"I just wondered how you put up with it," he muttered.

"I'm kind of used to it by now," I said. "I don't really notice any more."

That wasn't quite true, cos you can't help noticing. But I didn't want Tyler to think I was jealous or anything.

He seemed relieved that I wasn't offended. "I don't suppose," he said, "that you'd like to –"

His words were cut short by a sudden cry of, "Hey, Tyler!" It was Lola. "What are you doing here?" she said.

"Just on my way home," said Tyler. "Gotta go!"

We watched as he raced across the road and disappeared in the direction of Oak Avenue.

"What were you talking to him about?" said Lola.

"Just things," I said.

"What things?"

Lola sounded really put-out. She's not used to boys talking to me. But I was put-out, too. What had Tyler been going to say? *I don't suppose you'd like to* ... what? Thanks to my dear little sister, I would never know. Her and her pushy ways. I began to wonder how I *did* put up with her.

Next day, an envelope fluttered on to the front door mat. Lola pounced on it. And then she pouted and said, "Oh." She tossed it on to the hall table. "It's for you," she said.

I picked it up. It was addressed to "Miss Lucy French". Inside was a card. It was from Tyler! On the front was a picture of clogs. His handwriting was very neat and careful.

Hi Lucy

You rock! I don't suppose you would like to go out with me some time? Let me know. Give me a call.

Hope to see you soon.

Tyler

And then at the bottom he had written his phone number. I had never had a boy's phone number before!

Lola was jigging up and down, desperate to know who was writing to me.

"What is it?" she said. "Who is it from?"

"None of your business," I said.

"Oh! Well. If that's the way you feel." She tossed her hair back. "See if I care!"

And then she went wailing off down the hall. "Mu-u-um," she cried. "Lucy's got all big headed just cos she's in the next round!"

Chapter 8
Take a Bow

I had a secret. But I wasn't telling! Not just yet.

Mum and Lola couldn't talk about anything but the next round of auditions. They were, like, totally obsessed.

Lola would go, "Mum, you don't think pink tights with a pink tutu is a bit too pink, do you?"

And then Mum would go, "I wonder if we should dye the tutu and make it a bit darker? More like crimson, maybe."

And then we would all have to sit and watch while Lola went through her Sugar Plum dance for us. And then we would all have to listen while she rehearsed what she would say in her thank you speech if she won.

I tried not to be impatient cos I knew it was important for her. She kept telling me that it was.

"It's all right for you!" she cried. "It's just fun for you. But for me it's my whole life. Mum, tell her!"

I wondered if she was right about it just being fun for me. I decided that she probably was. The first audition hadn't been fun cos I had been too nervous. But something very odd had happened. Now that I'd reached the next round all my fears had vanished. Lola said that was because it wasn't really important to me.

"When it's important," she said, "you always have a bit of stage fright."

She said that she had *butterflies*. It's hard to believe when she is such a terrible show-off, but what did I know?

The day of the second round arrived. The auditions were being held in the same place as before, the Cornflower Studios, only this time there was an audience ...

Twenty of us were taking part. The girls I'd met at the first round hadn't made it, but the boy who played the spoons was there, and the girl who did street dancing. Much to Mum and Lola's disgust!

I did have a few butterflies when it was my turn to go on stage, but as soon as I started dancing they disappeared. I just pretended that I was back in Gran's kitchen, dancing for her and Grandad. And guess what? Guess what? I got Highly Commended! Same as Lola had got last year.

Grandad hugged me and said, "Your gran would be so proud of you."

Even Mum said, "Well done, Loopy!" and gave me a kiss.

Lola won first place. She had got through to the finals. She was going to be on television! I truly thought she deserved it. She had worked so hard, for so long. And it was so important to her. Plus her Sugar Plum Fairy was sweet as could be. I clapped as hard as anybody when she went up for her prize.

As soon as we got home, Mum went to the fridge and took out a special bottle of sparkly drink, which she had put in there "just in case". Lola and I both had a glass, and Mum and Grandad drank a toast to us.

"To our two little stars!"

"Only for the day," said Lola.

"Oh, come on!" said Mum. "What are you talking about? *Only for the day?*"

"Being a star doesn't last for ever," said Lola. She gave me this look. "If you want to keep on being a star you have to work at it."

"Oh, well. Yes, of course," Mum said. "I can't argue with that." And then she turned to me and said, "Does this mean you'll want to start dancing classes as well?"

I assured her that it didn't. I think Mum was quite relieved.

"Honestly," I said, "I wouldn't want to be a dancer. As a matter of fact," I added, as carelessly as I could, "I quite fancy being a doctor."

It was the first time I'd ever told anyone. I'd always had this feeling that Mum might laugh. *You?* she would go. *A doctor?* But she didn't.

Mum just said, "Oh!" She sounded a bit surprised. "Well, that's a good ambition to have. But you're still a star, even if it is only for a day. Let's make it two days ... let's all go up the road for a pizza tomorrow and have a proper celebration. How about that?"

The time had come to tell my secret.

"I can't tomorrow," I said.

They all turned to stare at me.

"Why's that?" said Mum.

I took a deep breath. "Cos I'm going out with Tyler," I said.

"Tyler?" Lola's eyes almost popped out of her head. "You've got a date with *Tyler*?"

"Why shouldn't she have?" said Mum. "No problem. We can go on Sunday."

"She won't still be a star by then," said Lola.

"Oh, I think she will," said Mum. "You both will!" And she put one arm round me and one arm round Lola and said, "You'll both always be stars as far as I'm concerned."

Grandad looked at me and winked. And I wondered which I was more excited about, being Highly Commended or going on a date with Tyler. Or maybe having a hug like that with Mum. I couldn't decide.

I guess this is what it must feel like to be a star!

Our books are tested
for children and young people by
children and young people.

Thanks to everyone who consulted on
a manuscript for their time and effort in
helping us to make our books better
for our readers.

*Also by **Jean Ure** ...*

Real True Friends

Hannah's the new girl at school.

It can be tricky making friends when everyone else knows each other.

Zoe Frost seems nice, and so does Michelle, the Queen of Cool. Problem is, Michelle won't be friends with Hannah if she's friends with Zoe ...

Will Hannah make the right choice and get her wish – a Real True Friend?

www.barringtonstoke.co.uk

More *fab stories* for girls ...

Cherry Green, Story Queen
ANNIE DALTON

Mia wishes she could leave the foster home and be back at home with her mum. But that's impossible.

But then Cherry Green arrives with a spring in her step and a book in her bag. Can one girl and one old book help Mia, Billy, Juno and Kyle find the happy ending they all need?

The Queen's Tale
KAYE UMANSKY

Three things Snow White's new stepmother is NOT a fan of:
1. Snow White
2. Snow White
3. Snow White

Skin as white as snow, hair as black as ebony and lips as red as blood?

How very last season.
Snow White has got to go.
It's poison apple time!

Sweetness and Lies
KAREN MCCOMBIE

New girl Amber is a champion ice-skater and visits her granny in Barbados.

Tilly's friend Mia thinks Amber is a total liar. Tilly and Mia have been friends since they started Beech Cliff School, so Tilly has to trust Mia. Right?

Or is Tilly about to do something very wrong?

The Cupcake Wedding
GILLIAN CROSS

Holly's sister Mia is going to marry her boyfriend James. But they're only 18. Are they too young to be married?

Soon all of Holly's friends and family have agreed to help out with the wedding. But Holly has her work cut out for her when the bride and groom both get cold feet!

www.barringtonstoke.co.uk